For Maureen, Aaron and Sean, and for Jon—loon lovers all. —J.L.

To my son Kelsey, who introduced me to the beautiful world of children's books, and special thanks to Scott for all his support and love. —S.F.

Text © 2002 by Jonathan London.
Illustrations © 2002 by Susan Ford.

Book design by Lucy Nielsen.
Typeset in Duckweed.
The illustrations in this book were rendered in pastel and gouache.
Manufactured in China.

Library of Congress Cataloging-in-Publication Data
London, Jonathan, 1947–
Loon Lake / by Jonathan London ; illustrated by Susan Ford.
p. cm.
Summary: A girl and her father encounter loons and other
lake creatures during a magical nighttime canoe ride.
ISBN 0-8118-2003-3
[1. Loons–Fiction. 2. Fathers and daughters–Fiction. 3. Lake animals–Fiction.
4. Lakes–Fiction.]   I. Ford, Susan, ill. II. Title.
PZ7.L8432 Lo 2001
[E]—dc21
00-008935

Distributed in Canada by Raincoast Books
9050 Shaughnessy Street, Vancouver, British Columbia V6P 6E5

10 9 8 7 6 5 4 3 2 1

Chronicle Books LLC
85 Second Street, San Francisco, California 94105

www.chroniclekids.com

Loon Lake

BY Jonathan London

ILLUSTRATED BY Susan Ford

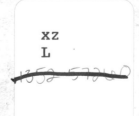
chronicle books · san francisco

Rain Bird, Rain Goose,
Call-up-a-Storm.

These are names
native people of the North
give to the loon.
That is what Papa tells me.

We watch the sun sink,
setting fire to the clouds,
and hear a loon's call.
I cup my hands
around my mouth
and try to make the loon's
crazy yodeling laugh.

Across Loon Lake,
Loon laughs back.

I've never seen a loon up close.

It's getting late,

but we set out to find him.

We ease our canoe

into the quiet northern lake

as the full moon rises

and spills a bright path

on the dark water.

We dip the blades of our paddles

—*dip glide dip glide*—

and slide through the moonlight

near the shore.

"There's an old Tsimshian story,"
Papa says, "about how Loon
got his white necklace."
I keep paddling as I listen.

"An old man had lost his sight and
asked for Loon's help," Papa says.
"Loon was a magical bird and
gave sight back to the old man.
And for this," says Papa,
"the old man gave Loon
his precious shell necklace.
The white shards of shell
adorn his feathers to this day."

In the moon shadows,

we see something move.

The slightest ripple.

I stop paddling, and so does Papa.

Our canoe glides,

and the something glides with us.

An otter!

His shiny nose and whiskers

arrow toward shore.

I glance back at Papa.

He puts a finger to his lips

and grins. We see a quick gleam

of moonlight on fur

as Otter slithers out of the water

and into low brush.

Again, something moves in the shadows.

Again, just a nose and whiskers,

dragging a soft ripple.

Buckteeth in the moonlight!

Beaver slaps his tail and goes under.

We start paddling.

Something else moves

in the shadowy water.

"A *loon!*" I whisper to Papa.

"A rain bird."

Slow, slow.

We paddle toward the loon.

But before we know it—

he's gone!

There! He rests in a nest
of stars on the still water.
We try to paddle closer
—*dip glide dip glide*—
but whenever we get too close
Loon quick-dives quietly . . .
and bobs up in another spot.

Now I glimpse him floating

behind a screen of reeds.

We paddle toward him,

silent as the moon.

He rears up, shakes his head,

flaps his wings . . .

then settles back down.

Fifty feet. Forty-five. Forty.

At thirty feet, we stop paddling.

Suddenly Loon glides out—
followed by another.
And another and another.

A *family!* I want to shout.
But I don't. Instead,
I hold my breath.

Whoosh! The loon family
takes off, running on water,
their splashes flashing white
in the moonlight.

I breathe deep,
and we turn back toward camp.

After supper,

around our campfire,

Papa whittles a stick sharp

and hands it to me.

I spear a marshmallow

and hold it over the flames

and imagine Loon and his family.

Just then, Loon's wild eerie wail

pierces the night.

I glance up and see a dark cloud

passing across the moon.

"Rain tonight," says Papa.

Later, we curl in our
sleeping bags and listen
to Loon's haunting cry—
and to the first drops of rain
as they tap against our tent.

Rain Bird, Rain Goose,
Call-up-a-Storm . . .

Good night.

Afterword

LOONS HAVE ALWAYS captivated the imaginations of humans. Their haunting wail, which can sound like a mad, yodeling laugh, has given rise to the expression "crazy as a loon" (and "loony"!). Native Americans have given them many names, including Rain Bird, Rain Goose and Call-up-a-Storm.

Also known as Great Northern Divers, loons are the best divers and swimmers of all flying birds. They can swim when they're only a few hours old, dive 240 feet deep and beat even the fastest trout in a race. Loon chicks are such good swimmers that they're sometimes called "water babies." But loons are clumsy on land, sometimes falling on their stomachs when they try to walk. The word *loon* comes from *lumme*—Old English for *lummox,* a clumsy person. Because they are so clumsy, loons only come ashore to nest.

Loons' ancestors lived 50 million years ago, almost as long ago as dinosaurs. They mate for life and will not share their lake with other loons, unless it's a very large lake where they can claim a bay as their own.

Loons lay their eggs—usually two or three—in early June. The male and female take turns sitting on the eggs, turning them with their bills to keep them evenly warm. After one month the chicks hatch, and when they are one week old they can dive and catch their own fish.

For six weeks the parents take good care of their "water babies." They help feed them, hide them along the shore and pop up in different places in the lake to attract the attention of predators—such as lynx and mink—away from them. When baby loons get tired, they often ride on their parents' backs.

Loons eat fish, frogs, crayfish, water plants, insects, even leeches. They propel themselves through the water with their paddlewheel feet, then "fly" under water, flapping their wings.

In late summer, adult loons shed their black-and-white checkered coats. By late September the chicks are almost full grown, and soon fly off with their parents to spend the winter on ice-free ocean coasts. They take off slowly, running wildly on the water's surface, but once they're in the air, they can fly 60 miles per hour.

Each spring, the loon parents return to the same northern lake, while their young find other lakes and look for mates of their own. Loons are very sensitive and are easily scared off. Their little lakes are home, and must be treated by us like precious eggs.

JIM ARNOSKY

Armadillo's Orange

G. P. PUTNAM'S SONS · NEW YORK

At the wild edge of an orange grove,
a young armadillo dug a burrow in soft, sandy soil.
Close by lay a big, round orange that had fallen
from its tree. The orange made it easy for
Armadillo to find his brand-new home.

Each day Armadillo left his burrow

to hunt for insects and grubs to eat.

He followed a narrow path

that wound its way

around the tangled stems

of plants and trees.

WITHDRAW

Every time he walked the winding path,

Armadillo passed beneath a lively green snake

climbing on a branch.

But Armadillo never looked up.

He just hurried on his way.

Down the path, a shy rattlesnake was coiled
in the shade of big, drooping leaves.
But Armadillo quickly waddled by,
looking only straight ahead.

Then an old, slow-moving tortoise

crossed the path.

Armadillo had to stop and wait.

He shuffled his feet impatiently

until the tortoise passed.

He hurried onto a fallen tree where he could dig
in the rotting wood for tasty grubs.

A scrub jay called out in its loud, raspy voice.
Armadillo closed his ears. Honeybees buzzed by
on their way to their hive.

Armadillo covered his face with his long claws.

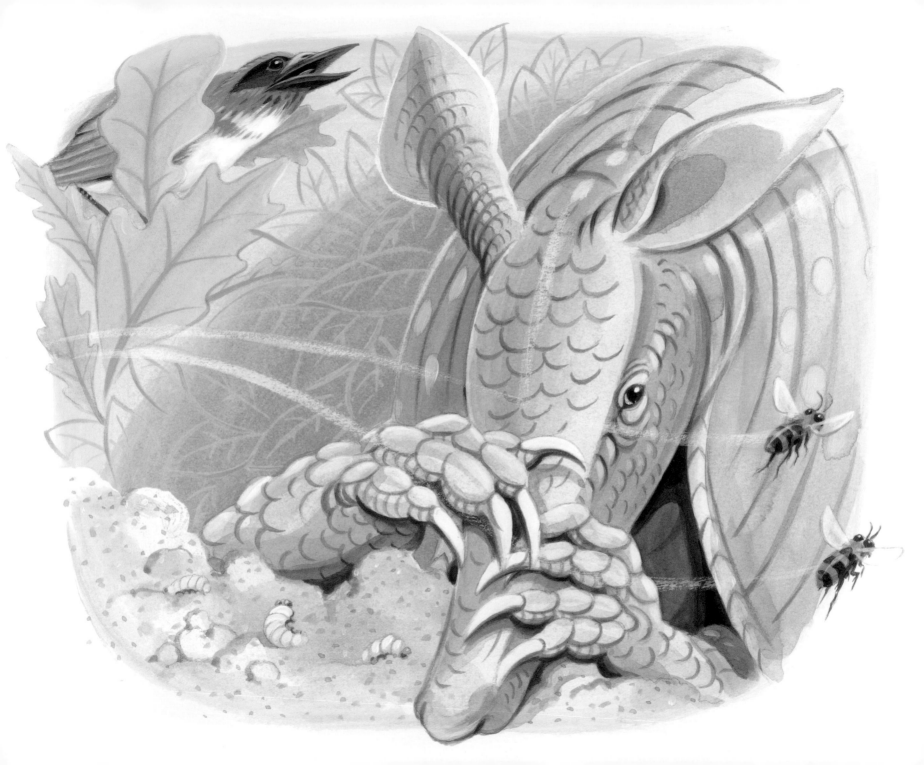

When the other animals had finally gone,

Armadillo gobbled up every grub

that he could find. Then he rushed back

down the path. When he saw the big, round orange,

he knew that he was home.

Every day was the same.

But one day, while Armadillo was away,

a sudden gust of wind blew through the grove.

The wind pushed Armadillo's orange

just enough to make it roll downhill into a weedy ditch.

When Armadillo returned, he could not find his burrow.

He walked and walked, looking for the orange

that marked the entrance to his home.

Everything seemed strange and wrong

with the big, round orange gone.

Armadillo wandered, lost and all alone.

Then, suddenly, he smelled the sweet scent of honeybees

and saw the old tortoise slowly crossing the path.

Together, Armadillo and Tortoise

watched the honeybees buzz by.

Then Armadillo heard the scrub jay
calling in its raspy voice. He followed the sound,
and soon he came upon the shy rattlesnake
resting in the shade. When Armadillo looked up,
he saw the lively green snake climbing on a branch.

Armadillo smelled and heard and saw these things
and knew that he was home.

Armadillo missed the big, round orange

shining brightly near his hole.

But with neighbors living all around,

he didn't need it anymore.

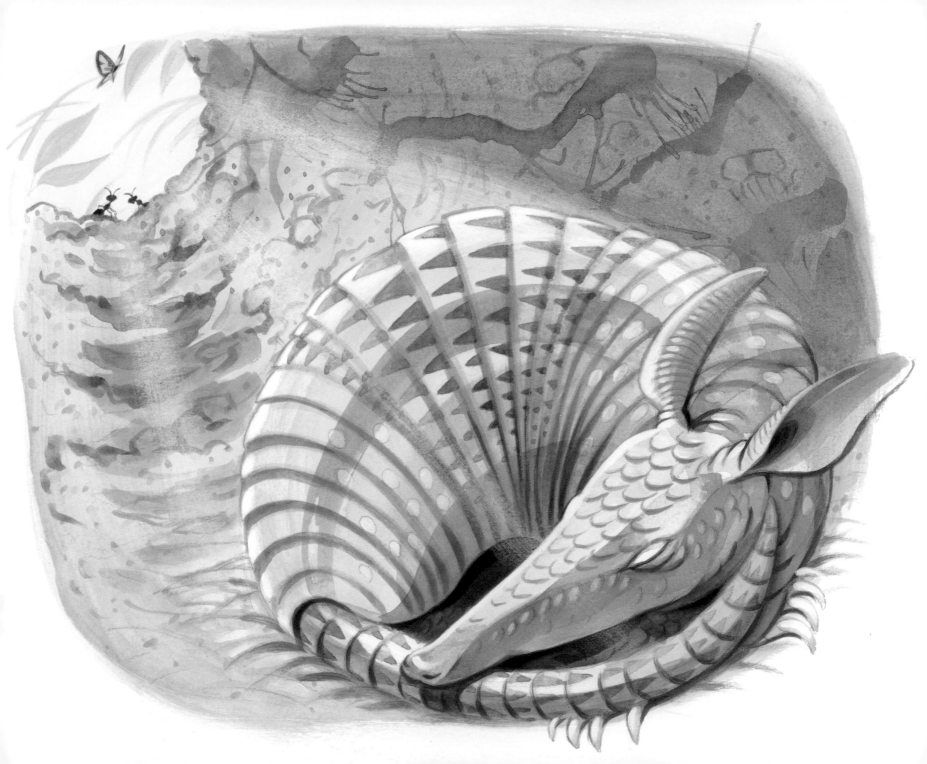